Kanchil Outsmarts the Crocodile

A Folktale from Malaysia and Indonesia

CHARACTERS
IN ORDER OF APPEARANCE

Budi

the head crocodile

Arti

Budi's crocodile friend

Kersen

Budi's crocodile friend

Santoso

Budi's crocodile friend

Kanchil

a mouse deer

Kade

Kanchil's water buffalo friend

SETTING

A riverbank near a jungle
in Southeast Asia

Budi: I'm telling you, fellas, I've had enough of that Kanchil playing tricks on us crocodiles. I'm going to put an end to it once and for all!

Arti: What are you going to do, boss?

Kersen: Yeah, that mouse deer is pretty smart, especially for someone who isn't a crocodile.

Budi: He's not that smart.

Arti: Oh no? Remember that time he pretended to put his leg in the water for you to eat, but it was actually just a stick?

Kersen: Or how about that time you pretended to be a log? You were going to capture Kanchil when he stepped on you.

Santoso: Except Kanchil said, "Well, if it's a log, it won't talk," and you said, "Of course I'm a log." You gave it away—and Kanchil got away.

Budi: Well, it won't happen again. I am going to capture that crafty mouse deer and end his trickery.

Arti: Speaking of that mouse deer, there he is now.

Budi: He won't get me this time because *I* am going to do the getting.

Kanchil: Good day and *salaam*, my crocodile friends!

Crocodiles: Hello, good day, and *salaam* to you, too.

Budi: (*arrogantly*) What are you doing on my riverbank, pip-squeak?

Kanchil: I'm here on official business from the king.

Budi: (*humbly*) The king? The king? What does the king want from us?

Arti: Does he need us to open cans with our razor-sharp teeth?

Kersen: Would he like to clean his boots on our spiky backs?

Santoso: Would he like us to transport his boat down the river? We'll do anything for the king.

Kanchil: He's asked me to count all the crocodiles. I'm not sure why. Maybe he wants to give a present to all the crocodiles and needs to know how many gifts to get.

Budi: A gift? From the king? So he finally wants to show how much he appreciates all we do for him.

Kanchil: Yes, well, it's hard to count you when you're all mixed around. Line up across the river so I can count you more easily.

Budi: You heard him, fellas. Line up!

Arti: Yes, boss, I'm on my way, ready for action.

Kersen: Anything for our great and mighty king. We are his loyal subjects.

Santoso: I hope it's a big, humongous present!

Budi: We're lined up across the river. Now what?

Kanchil: I'll just step on each of your backs so I'm sure I count *each one* of you. Here I go. One . . .

Arti: Number one! That's me! That's right, baby!

Kanchil: Two . . .

Kersen: Hey! I want to be number one! Why can't I be number one? He's always number one!

Budi: Quiet! Continue, Kanchil. We must not keep the king waiting!

Kanchil: Three . . .

Santoso: (*imagining to himself*) A brand new hat . . . a shiny gold watch . . . an electric toothbrush . . .

Kanchil: And four. And . . . now I'm across the river! Thanks for your help! See you later, alligators.

Arti: We're crocodiles, right, boss? He said "alligators." Guess he's not that smart after all.

Budi: Quiet! Where are you going, Kanchil? What about the king?

Kanchil: You fell for my trick! I only wanted to get to the tasty fruits on this side of the river. I didn't know how I would get across. But thanks to you and your friends making a crocodile bridge, I am here. Good-bye. See you in awhile, crocodiles.

Arti: That's better . . . "crocodiles" . . . right, boss?

Budi: No, it isn't! He tricked us again.

Kersen: He's smooth, you can't deny it. Smooth as a set of silk sheets, I tell ya.

Santoso: I want my present!

Budi: Be quiet! I vow that this will never happen to me again! I will get that Kanchil yet! All I need is a good night's sleep. I'll rest my mind . . . make new plans . . . Zzzzz!

Arti, Kersen, and **Santoso:** Nap time! Zzzzz . . .

Kanchil: *(to the audience)* Another beautiful day has dawned, bringing another opportunity to play a trick on Budi the crocodile! Hee hee! Wait until you see the new trick I have for him today. *(to Budi)* Hello, Budi!

Budi: Kanchil, I've had enough of you and your tricks. I'm going to capture you—and eat you!

Kanchil: Today? Now? This isn't a good time for me to be eaten. I'm watching the king's pudding.

Budi: *(hopefully)* The king? *(skeptically)* Wait a minute. I'm not falling for that trick this time.

Kanchil: Take that chance, but I wouldn't want to be *you* when the king finds out that his pudding got ruined because of *you.* Capture me if you must.

Budi: Well . . . hmm . . . I certainly don't want the king to be upset with me. Maybe I'll wait until tomorrow to get you—if you let me taste the pudding.

Kanchil: Oh, I couldn't do that. It belongs to the king. Too bad. It looks so rich and chocolaty.

Budi: Chocolate pudding? I love chocolate pudding! Give me a taste!

Kanchil: I would if I could, but the king has trusted me with it.

Budi: Oh, come on. Pretty please? I *must* have some. Give me a taste *right now* or our deal is off!

Kanchil: Okay, but you must not tell a soul. Here it is.

Budi: But that looks like a mud puddle.

Kanchil: Then don't taste it and let me bring it to the king.

Budi: Wait! Let me try a taste ... Ptooey! This *is* a mud puddle! Bleh! You've tricked me again!

Kanchil: Good day, my muddy-mouthed friend!

Budi: I'll get you yet, Kanchil!

Arti: Budi, you're covered in mud from tail to snout.

Kersen: We saw what Kanchil did to you! Oh boy, what a belly laugh I had! I thought I would bust a gut ... Oops, sorry, boss.

Santoso: It sure *looked* like chocolate pudding. Do you have any left?

Budi: This is the last straw! I will never fall for a Kanchil trick again. He makes me so angry. And when I am angry, I get hungry.

Arti: Hey, look over there. It's Kade, the water buffalo, coming our way. She's not crafty like Kanchil.

Kersen: She would make a hearty meal for some hungry crocodiles.

Budi: Stand back. We're going to feast on water buffalo today.

Santoso: But I was in the mood for delicious chocolate pudding.

Budi: Quiet! I have an idea how we can get her. Quick—put this log on top of me. Then go hide.

Kanchil: *(to audience)* It's good that I'm small. Those mean crocodiles don't see me hiding here in the tall grass. So, Budi is trying to get my friend Kade. I won't let that happen!

Budi: Good day and *salaam*, Kade! Could I ask for some assistance, please? As you can see, this log has fallen on me and I am quite stuck.

Kade: Um . . . *Salaam*, Budi. Sorry about your troubles, but I cannot help you. I am afraid you will eat me.

Budi: I can understand your hesitation, my dear, since I am a crocodile. But I would certainly never harm someone who would help me in such a way.

Kade: Budi, I cannot help you today—or any day for that matter. Your sharp teeth and mischievous grin make me uneasy.

Budi: Please. My back is breaking. I would be too weak to capture you, anyway.

11

Kade: You're probably right. Okay, I'll help. After all, you are a fellow creature in need.

Budi: Delicious . . . I mean, wonderful. Now pull!

Kade: It's becoming looser . . . almost there . . . I feel it starting to budge . . . there! I've removed it.

Budi: Thank you! And now, to show my appreciation, I'll . . . grab you! You'll make a lovely lunch.

Kade: But Budi, you can't. You promised!

Budi: You should know never to trust a crocodile.

Kade: Help! Oh, somebody, please help me!

Kanchil: What's going on here, Budi?

Budi: Kanchil, I was just about to have my lunch. I could use some dessert. You! Come a little closer.

Kade: Help me, Kanchil! Budi tricked me!

Kanchil: How did you get captured?

Kade: Budi said if I helped him push a log off his back, he wouldn't eat me. So I helped him.

Kanchil: That was foolish. You should know never to trust a crocodile.

Budi: My words exactly.

Kanchil: Kade, I guess you deserve to be eaten.

Kade: What? You cannot be serious! I thought we were friends!

Budi: Kanchil, *you* are betraying a friend?

Kanchil: Well, I like my friends to be clever, and Kade fell for your trick. So she deserves to be eaten.

Kade: Kanchil, no! After all we've been through?

Kanchil: I do love your friendship, Kade, but I love cleverness even more. So, this is what must happen.

Budi: I'm glad you finally see things my way, Kanchil.

Kanchil: I was just wondering, though, how did you do it, Budi? I'm having a hard time picturing it.

Budi: So you're not as clever as you think. Well, I put the log on my back . . .

Kanchil: Wait, I really can't imagine it. Could you act it out for me? Just so I can see for myself how clever you were.

Budi: Well, yes, I am quite proud of myself. Okay. Kade, wait right here. I'll be back to eat you. Now, I asked my buddies to place this big log on my back.

Kanchil: Like this?

Budi: Yes, they put it across my back just like that, so I couldn't move. Then I . . .

Kanchil: Are you sure you can't move?

Budi: Absolutely. (*grunts*) See?

Kanchil: Yes, I see. *You* can't move—but *we* can! Come on, Kade, let's go!

Kade: Oh, Kanchil, I had a hunch you were playing a trick on Budi!

Budi: What? A trick? It can't be! It can't be!

Kanchil: It can be and it is, Budi.

Budi: Arti! Kersen! Santoso! Help me!

Kanchil: Let's go, Kade.

Kade: I'm already ahead of you! Thanks for helping me out of a jam.

Kanchil: Hey, what are friends for? Now let's get out of here before Budi gets that log off himself!

Budi: I'll get you, Kanchil. If it's the last thing I do, I'll get you!

Arti: Boss, why is the log still on you? What happened?

Budi: Never mind what happened. Just get this log off me.

Kersen: Sure thing, boss. Ooof! It's heavy . . . here goes . . . almost there . . . ahhh!

Budi: There. That's better. Now, we will never speak of this again. Do you hear me?

Santoso: Okay, boss. I have just one teensy-weensy, itsy-bitsy little question, though.

Budi: What's that?

Santoso: Did you happen to save any water buffalo meat for us?

Budi: That's it! Get away from me! I tell you, I will get that Kanchil! I will! It may not be today. It may not be tomorrow. But mark my words, he will be gotten. All I need is the right plan . . .

The End